CW01018856

Let's have a Story

Let's have a Story

compiled by

NERYS HUGHES

illustrated by

DAVID ARTHUR

HUTCHINSON
London Melbourne Sydney Auckland Johannesburg

Hutchinson Children's Books Ltd
An imprint of the Hutchinson Publishing Group
17–21 Conway Street, London W1P 6JD

Hutchinson Publishing Group (Australia) Pty Ltd
PO Box 496, 16–22 Church Street, Hawthorne, Melbourne,
Victoria 3122

Hutchinson Group (NZ) Ltd
32–34 View Road, PO Box 40-086, Glenfield, Auckland 10

Hutchinson Group (SA) Pty Ltd
PO Box 337, Bergvlei 2012, South Africa

First published 1984

Set in Baskerville by BookEns, Saffron Walden, Essex

Printed and bound in Great Britain by Anchor Brendon Ltd,
Tiptree, Essex

ISBN 0 09 156770 X

Contents

Introduction

Isn't reading a good story one of the very best ways to spend your time? It can be very exciting and stimulating – quite often I cannot put a really good book down, and find myself at three in the morning, red-eyed and spent, reading the last page of a novel when I only meant to read a chapter! When I was a child, I remember reading illicitly after 'lights out', and being blissfully terrified by science fiction and horror stories. But perhaps the best part of reading is the friendship of a book; the familiarity of a loved story, or identifying with a special person in a story.

My daughter, Mari-Claire, is five years old and can read some books for herself now, but I think it will be some time before we forfeit that shared time snuggled up enjoying a good story together.

With this collection, Mari-Claire and I would like to introduce you to some of our friends – such as Wriggly Worm, Gilbert the Ostrich and good old Uncle Charlie with his ramshackle car – and share with you some of our favourite stories. We hope you like them!

Nerys Hughes

The Elephant's Picnic

RICHARD HUGHES

Elephants are generally clever animals, but there was once an elephant who was very silly; and his great friend was a kangaroo. Now, kangaroos are not often clever animals, and this one certainly was not, so she and the elephant got on very well together.

One day they thought they would like to go off for a picnic by themselves. But they did not know anything about picnics, and had not the faintest idea of what to do to get ready.

'What do you do on a picnic?' the elephant asked a child he knew.

'Oh, we collect wood and make a fire, and then we boil the kettle,' said the child.

'What do you boil the kettle for?' said the elephant in surprise.

'Why, for tea, of course,' said the child in a snapping sort of way; so the elephant did not like to ask any more questions. But he went and told the kangaroo, and they collected together all the things they thought they would need.

When they got to the place where they were going to have their picnic, the kangaroo said that she would collect the wood because she had got a pouch to carry it back in. A kangaroo's pouch, of course, is very small; so the kangaroo carefully chose the smallest twigs she could find, and only about five or six of those. In fact, it took a lot of hopping to find any sticks small enough to go in her pouch at all; and it was a long time before she came back. But silly though the elephant was, he soon saw those sticks would not be enough for a fire.

'Now *I* will go off and get some wood,' he said.

His ideas of getting wood were very different. Instead of taking little twigs he pushed down whole trees with his forehead, and staggered back to the picnic-place with them rolled up in his trunk. Then the kangaroo struck a match, and they lit a bonfire made of whole trees. The blaze, of course, was enormous, and the fire so hot that for a long time they could not get near it; and it was not until it began to die down a bit that they were able to get near enough to cook anything.

'Now let's boil the kettle,' said the elephant. Amongst the things he had brought was a brightly shining copper kettle and a very large

black iron saucepan. The elephant filled the saucepan with water.

'What are you doing that for?' said the kangaroo.

'To boil the kettle in, you silly,' said the elephant. So he popped the kettle in the saucepan of water, and put the saucepan on the fire; for he thought, the old juggins, that you boil a kettle in the same sort of way you boil an egg, or boil a cabbage! And the kangaroo, of course, did not know any better.

So they boiled and boiled the kettle, and every now and then they prodded it with a stick.

'It doesn't seem to be getting tender,' said the elephant sadly, 'and I am sure we can't eat it for tea until it does.'

So then away he went and got more wood for the fire; and still the saucepan boiled and boiled, and still the kettle remained as hard as ever. It was getting late now, almost dark.

'I am afraid it won't be ready for tea,' said the kangaroo, 'I am afraid we shall have to spend the night here. I wish we had got something with us to sleep in.'

'Haven't you?' said the elephant. 'You mean to say you didn't pack before you came away?'

'No,' said the kangaroo. 'What should I have packed, anyway?'

'Why, your trunk, of course,' said the elephant. 'That is what people pack.'

'But I haven't got a trunk,' said the kangaroo.

'Well, I have,' said the elephant, 'and I've packed it. Kindly pass the pepper; I want to unpack!'

So then the kangaroo passed the elephant the pepper, and the elephant took a good sniff. Then he gave a most enormous sneeze, and everything he had packed in his trunk shot out of it – toothbrush, spare socks, gym shoes, a comb, a bag of bull's-eyes, his pyjamas, and his Sunday suit. So then the elephant put on his pyjamas and lay down to sleep; but the kangaroo had no pyjamas, and so, of course, she could not possibly sleep.

'All right,' she said to the elephant; 'you sleep and I will sit up and keep the fire going.'

So all night the kangaroo kept the fire blazing

brightly and the kettle boiling merrily in the saucepan. When the next morning came the elephant woke up.

'Now,' he said, 'let's have our breakfast.'

So they took the kettle out of the saucepan; and what do you think? *It was boiled as tender as tender could be!* So they cut it fairly in half and shared it between them, and ate it for their breakfast; and both agreed they had never had so good a breakfast in their lives.

Wriggley Worm and the New Pet

EUGENIE SUMMERFIELD

One lazy day in June, Wriggly Worm was lying in the long grass enjoying the scent of flowers all round him. Anthea Ant came bustling along.

'Ah, there you are, Wriggly,' she said, 'I've something important to say to you.'

'Yes?' said Wriggly.

Anthea settled down beside him. 'I'm worried about Cirencester,' she began.

'Oh, not again!' groaned Wriggly. Cirencester, the sad stick insect, was a constant problem.

'How can anyone stop him from being sad for very long?'

'Ah-ha!' said Anthea, looking pleased with herself, 'I think I know the answer to that question.'

'You do?' Wriggly was glad to hear this.

'He's sad,' went on Anthea, 'because he needs someone to love him. And someone he can love too.'

'But, Anthea, we're his friends. We love him,' said Wriggly.

'Yes, yes, I know, but it's not the same as having someone or something of his very own.'

Then Wriggly Worm had a wonderful idea. 'What Cirencester needs is a pet,' he said.

Anthea wasn't so sure at first. She had never heard of a stick insect having a pet. She asked Wriggly Worm, 'What kind of a pet should it be, Wriggly? He'll need something quiet and friendly.'

Wriggly Worm went down into his secret tunnel to have a think about this. Then up he came, all excited.

'I've got it, Anthea! Leave it to me. I'll find Cirencester a nice quiet pet he can love.'

Anthea was delighted. 'Thank you, Wriggly. You are wonderful,' she said. 'Now I must go. I've got so much else to do.'

Wriggly Worm knew where there was a lost pet who would just suit Cirencester. And as soon as Wriggly had found it, he sent it round to Cirencester right away.

So, later on, it was no surprise to Wriggly Worm when a note arrived by pigeon post which said: 'Please come to a special picnic today to meet my new pet. Lots of lettuce for tea. Love Cirencester. P.S. And thank you, Wriggly.'

Everybody had had notes by pigeon post that day. Sloppy Slug, Brown Snail, all the little Brown Snails, and Anthea Ant had all been invited. The little Brown Snails were all smart and shiny, ready for the picnic. Sloppy Slug was looking forward to lettuce for tea. He hoped it wouldn't all be eaten up before he got there. 'I think we'd better hurry,' he said. 'We don't want to be late for tea.'

'Wriggly,' said Brown Snail, as they crawled along together, 'what sort of a pet will it be?'

'Ah! yes, well . . .' said Wriggly, because he knew. 'You'll have to wait and see.'

All the way along the little Brown Snails played guessing games. They were trying to find out what Cirencester's pet could be.

'It couldn't be an ant or an elephant.'

'It couldn't be a quail or a little Brown Snail.'

16

'Could it be a squirrel, with a big bushy tail?'

'Tell us, Wriggly. Tell us what it'll be.'

'No, no, no! You wait and see. Whatever it is, it will make Cirencester happy.'

Everyone was pleased about that. So, what a shock they all got when they reached Cirencester's special part of the garden and found him crying.

'Oh, woe, woe is me! Oh, why do sad things always happen to *me*? Oh, woe, oh, woe!'

Wriggly Worm hurried forward.

'Whatever's the matter, Cirencester?' he asked. 'We didn't expect to find you in tears.'

There was Cirencester sitting hunched up on a huge smooth brown stone, sobbing. 'I've lost him! I've lost my new pet,' he cried.

'We'll look for him,' said Wriggly. 'Everybody look for Cirencester's new pet.'

'Yes, yes,' cried all the little Brown Snails. They began to scurry hither and thither.

Then one called out, 'Wriggly, tell us what we're looking for?'

'Well,' Wriggly replied, 'his name's Shy. He's brown and smooth and rather like that huge thing Cirencester's sitting on –' He stopped suddenly. Then he said, 'Cirencester! You old silly, you're sitting on your new pet tortoise. You

17

haven't lost him at all!'

Cirencester jumped down and hopped round to one end where there was quite a pile of lettuce leaves. A head came out of the shell and said in a whisper, 'Hello, I'm Shy.' And then popped back in again.

'He's very friendly really,' explained Cirencester, 'when he gets used to people.'

And he was. He gave the little Brown Snails rides on his back. He told them tortoise stories they had never heard before. They all had a lovely picnic. Everyone enjoyed it, especially Cirencester.

18

Charlie Finds a Pet

MARGARET GREAVES

'Now, Charlie,' said Miss Mansfield, 'it's your turn to tell us something today.'

Charlie White stared glumly at the class and said nothing.

'Well, what did you do on Saturday, dear?'

'Nothing,' said Charlie.

'Everybody does something,' said Miss Mansfield. 'Perhaps you could talk about your pet.'

'Haven't got a pet,' said Charlie.

Miss Mansfield gave up.

'Sandra, I can see you've got something to tell us.'

Sandra told them a lot about her birthday. Nobody took much notice except Peter, who wanted to talk about the train set he'd had for *his* birthday.

Charlie walked home with Emma at the end of the day. They both lived in the same road as the school. Emma lived in the last house and Charlie next door to her.

Charlie kicked a stone out of his way.

'Miss Mansfield asks silly questions,' he said. 'But I wish I had got a pet.'

'Why don't you have one?'

'Mum says there's no room. And they make a mess.'

'You can have a share in our Bob if you like,' offered Emma.

Bob was a big ginger tom cat who belonged to Emma's family. He was the terror of all the other cats in the road.

'Thanks,' said Charlie. 'But we sort of share him already. He digs as many holes in our garden as he does in yours.'

Workmen had been busy in the road while the children were at school. They had made a huge hole and roped it off and left it.

'Let's look,' said Emma.

They hung on to the rope and looked in. There were big pipes at the bottom and a lot of mud.

'I expect it's gas,' said Charlie.

'Perhaps it's water. If it's water it might burst,' said Emma hopefully. 'There was one in the High Street and it made a huge spout of water and everyone got wet.'

Charlie hoped that it was water too, but he didn't want Emma to be too cocky.

'It's gas,' he said.

'Oh look!' said Emma. 'There's something moving down there.'

So there was! A small live something was crawling up out of the mud at the bottom. It had a long head and narrow body and a very long tail and four very short legs. At first it looked almost the same colour as the mud. But as it came up into the sun it shone a bright, bright green.

'It's a lizard,' said Charlie. 'Hold me.'

He ducked his head under the rope and leaned into the hole as far as he could. Emma held on to the seat of his pants. He picked up the lizard and wriggled back with it. It sat quite still in Charlie's hand and looked at them with small red eyes. It had a bright red mark on each shoulder too, and there was a line of sky-blue scales along its back.

'Isn't he lovely?' said Emma.

'He likes me,' said Charlie. 'I shall keep him as a pet.'

'I saw him first,' said Emma.

'But I knew he was a lizard and you didn't. And I picked him up. He's mine.' Then Charlie remembered that Emma had kindly offered him a share in Bob, the ginger cat. 'All right, you can share him too. But I'll keep him.'

'All right,' said Emma. 'I'm glad you've got a pet. What will you call him?'

'Alberic,' said Charlie. The name came to him quite suddenly. He didn't know where he'd heard it. But it sounded fierce. And the lizard looked fierce too, although he was so small.

'You'd better put him in your pocket,' said Emma, 'in case he runs away.'

But the lizard opened his mouth with a hiss, and they saw two rows of sharp white teeth.

'He doesn't like pockets,' said Charlie.

So Emma fished out a paper bag that she'd had for some biscuits, and they put him in that.

'See you later,' said Charlie, when they reached his gate. 'I'll bring him round to your house after tea.'

He went in, whistling. He'd got a pet of his own at last.

The Billy-Goats Gruff

RETOLD BY LEILA BERG

Once upon a time there were three billy-goats Gruff. They were all called Gruff. That was their name.

At the end of their field was a hill, and the billy-goats Gruff liked to go up the hillside to eat the juicy green grass and make themselves fat.

But to get to the hill they had to cross a bridge that went over a little river; and under the bridge lived a troll, with eyes as big as saucers and a nose as long as a poker.

Now one day the three billy-goats Gruff decided to go up the hillside to make themselves fat. First came the youngest billy-goat Gruff, trip-trap, on to the bridge.

'Who's that running on to my bridge?' roared the troll.

'It's only me, the littlest billy-goat Gruff. I'm just going on to the hillside to make myself fat.'

'Don't you dare to come on to my bridge, or I'll gobble you up!'

'Oh, don't gobble me up. I'm much too little. Eat my big brother. He's just coming now.'

'Oh, all right,' said the troll.

So the youngest billy-goat Gruff ran, trip-trap, right over the bridge and on to the hillside.

Presently along came the second billy-goat Gruff, trip-trap-trip, on to the bridge.

'Who's that running on to my bridge?' roared the troll.

'Oh, it's only me, the second billy-goat Gruff. I'm just going up the hillside to make myself fat.'

'Don't you dare come on to my bridge, or I'll gobble you up!'

'Oh, don't gobble me up. I'm much too little. Eat my big brother instead. He's just coming now.'

'Oh, all right,' said the troll.

So the second billy-goat Gruff ran, trip-trap-trip, right over the bridge and on to the hillside.

Presently along came the biggest billy-goat Gruff, trip-trap-trip-trap, on to the bridge.

'Who's that running on to my bridge?' roared the troll.

'It's me, the biggest billy-goat Gruff. I'm going up the hillside to make myself fat.'

'Don't you dare come on to my bridge,' roared the troll, 'or I'll gobble you up!'

'Gobble me up!' said the biggest billy-goat Gruff. 'Gobble me up! Oh no you won't!' And he ran at the troll with his long horns, and he tossed him up in the air, and he tossed him down in the water. Then he went over the bridge, trip-trap-trip-trap, and on to the hillside to join his brothers. And all the three billy-goats Gruff ate the juicy green grass, till they were so fat they could scarcely get home again.

The Little Wooden Horse

URSULA MORAY WILLIAMS

One day Uncle Peder made a little wooden horse. This was not at all an extraordinary thing, for Uncle Peder made toys every day of his life, but oh, this was such a brave little horse, so gay and splendid on his four green wheels, so proud and dashing with his red saddle and blue stripes! Uncle Peder had never made so fine a little horse before.

'I shall ask five shillings for this little wooden horse!' he cried.

What was his surprise when he saw large tears trickling down the newly painted face of the little wooden horse.

'Don't do that!' said Uncle Peder. 'Your paint will run. And what is there to cry about? Do you want more spots on your sides? Do you wish for bigger wheels? Do you creak? Are you stiff? Aren't your stripes broad enough? Upon my word I can see nothing to cry about! I shall certainly sell you for five shillings!'

But the tears still ran down the newly painted
cheeks of the little wooden horse, till at last
Uncle Peder lost patience. He picked him up
and threw him on the pile of wooden toys he
meant to sell in the morning. The little wooden
horse said nothing at all, but went on crying.
When night came and the toys slept in the sack
under Uncle Peder's chair the tears were still
running down the cheeks of the little wooden
horse.

In the morning Uncle Peder picked up the
sack and set out to sell his toys.

At every village he came to the children ran
out to meet him, crying 'Here's Uncle Peder!

Here's Uncle Peder come to sell his wooden toys!'

Then out of the cottages came the mothers and the fathers, the grandpas and the grandmas, the uncles and the aunts, the elder cousins and the godparents, to see what Uncle Peder had to sell.

The children who had birthdays were very fortunate: they had the best toys given to them, and could choose what they would like to have. The children who had been good in school were lucky, too. Their godparents bought them wooden pencil-boxes and rulers and paper-cutters, like grown-up people. The little ones had puppets, dolls, marionettes and tops. Uncle Peder had made them all, painting the dolls in red and yellow, the tops in blue, scarlet and green. When the children had finished choosing, their mothers, fathers, grandpas, grandmas, uncles, aunts, elder cousins, and godparents sent them home, saying, 'Now let's hear no more of you for another year!' Then they stayed behind to gossip with old Peder, who bought them news from the other villages he had passed by on his way.

Nobody bought the little wooden horse, for nobody had five shillings to spend. The fathers and the mothers, the grandpas and the grandmas, the uncles and the aunts, the elder cousins and the godparents, all shook their heads, saying,

'Five shillings! Well, that's too much! Won't you take any less, Uncle Peder?'

But Uncle Peder would not take a penny less.

'You see, I have never made such a fine little horse before,' he said.

All the while the tears ran down the nose of the little wooden horse, who looked very sad indeed, so that when Uncle Peder was alone once more he asked him, 'Tell me, my little wooden horse, what is there to cry about? Have I driven the nails crookedly into your legs? Don't you like your nice green wheels and your bright blue stripes? What is there to cry about, I'd like to know?'

At last the little wooden horse made a great effort and sobbed out, 'Oh, master, I don't want to leave you! I'm a quiet little horse, I don't want to be sold. I want to stay with you for ever and ever, I shouldn't cost much to keep, master. Just a little bit of paint now and then; perhaps a little oil in my wheels once a year. I'll serve you faithfully, master, if only you won't sell me for five shillings. I'm a quiet little horse, I am, and the thought of going out into the wide world breaks my heart. Let me stay with you here, master – oh, do!'

Uncle Peder scratched his head as he looked in surprise at his little wooden horse.

'Well,' he said, 'that's a funny thing to cry about! Most of my toys want to go out into the wide world. Still, as nobody wants to give five shillings for you, and you have such a melancholy expression, you can stop with me for the present, and maybe I won't get rid of you after all.'

When Uncle Peder said this the little wooden horse stopped crying at once, and galloped three times round in a circle.

'Why, you're a gay fellow after all!' said Uncle Peder, as the little wooden horse kicked his legs in the air, so that the four green wheels spun round and round.

Uncle Peder and the little wooden horse became great friends.

'Who would have thought it?' said Uncle Peder.

Thomas and the Monster

MARJORIE STANNARD

Thomas put on his wellies and his lucky woollen hat and walked up the garden path.

'I see you've got your lucky hat on,' remarked Snoodles the tortoise, who was just waking up from a nap on the grass. 'Are you going somewhere special?'

'Just looking for Monsters,' said Thomas. 'There might be one at the bottom, where the stream is.'

'Well, don't shout for me if you find one,' said Snoodles sleepily. 'I'm just going to have another little sleep in the rhubarb patch.'

Thomas walked on under the cherry trees until he came to the little summer-house by the stream. It was very quiet down here. The stream was half dried up and only made a soft murmur as it ran and the birds only twittered now and then because they were resting in green branches away from the hot sun.

He walked round the summer-house and

looked in through its small dusty window. He couldn't see very well because the dust was quite thick, so he rubbed the glass with his lucky woollen hat.

Then he looked again. Inside was a wooden table with two chairs. On the table lay a heap of red cherries. And sitting on one of the chairs was a Monster.

Thomas knew he was a Monster because his hair was green and very short, like fur; and he had two horns sticking out – one above each ear.

Thomas put on his lucky hat again and opened the door.

'Hallo,' he said, 'are you a Monster?'

The Monster looked rather frightened. 'I hope you don't mind me being here,' he said nervously in a kind of choky voice, as though he had a sore throat. 'I couldn't find anywhere else to sleep. And I had a few cherries.'

Thomas sat down on the other chair. 'I don't mind at all,' he said. And he gave the Monster a handful of cherries and took some himself.

'I was on my want back to the mountains,' the Monster explained, putting his cherry-stones neatly in a row, 'when somehow I took a wrong turning. I got mixed up with motorways and railway stations and yards full of buses. Nobody saw me because I'm rather good at dodging underneath things. In the end I found myself in your garden. I am quite worn out. So I had a drink of stream-water and a few cherries, and came in here.'

'You can stay as long as you want,' said Thomas kindly. 'Which mountains are you going to?'

'This year,' said the Monster, 'I'm going to Wales. My uncle told me of a nice dry cave by a lake that will just suit me.'

'I think my Dad's got a map of England and Wales,' said Thomas, looking excited. 'Wait here for me.' And he ran up the path into the house. Thomas went into the kitchen and asked Mum if he could borrow the map for a little while. Mum got it out of the bureau drawer for him.

'Be careful with it,' said Mum, 'and put it back in the drawer when you've finished.'

Thomas carried the map down to the garden shed and spread it out on the table so that the Monster could see it properly. After a little while he said happily, 'Now I see where I went wrong! Do you mind if I take a few cherries in my pocket? Thank you very much. I'll be on my way now. And if ever you come to that lake in North Wales I showed you, be sure to look me up. My relations will all be very pleased to meet you. I suppose,' he added, blinking his rather beautiful green eyes, 'I suppose you wouldn't let me try

on your hat before I go?'

Thomas was a little doubtful if it would fit him, as he had a couple of horns to manage; but when Thomas passed it over he put it on his head quite easily, letting the horns poke through on each side.

'It *does* feel nice and warm,' said the Monster, giving a sort of sigh. And he was just going to take it off when Thomas said suddenly, 'No, you keep it. It's a lucky hat, so I'm sure you'll get to Wales all right.'

The Monster beamed. 'I'll be off, then. Good-bye!'

And he hurried through the door and disappeared among the bushes.

Thomas folded the map up carefully. Then he looked at the Monster's cherry-stones lying in a neat row.

'I'll keep them,' said Thomas to himself. 'Then nobody can say I haven't really seen a Monster.'

When he got back to the kitchen Mum said, 'Where's your lucky hat?'

'I've lent it to a Monster,' said Thomas.

'Well,' said Mum, 'it was time you had a new one, anyway.'

And that very evening she started to knit him a new one.

How the Camel got its Hump

RUDYARD KIPLING

In the beginning of years, when the world was so new-and-all, and the Animals were just beginning to work for Man, there was a Camel, and he lived in the middle of a Howling Desert because he did not want to work; and besides, he was a Howler himself. So he ate sticks and thorns and tamarisks and milkweed and prickles, most 'scrutiating idle; and when anybody spoke to him he said 'Humph!' Just 'Humph!' and no more.

Presently the Horse came to him on Monday morning, with a saddle on his back and a bit in his mouth, and said, 'Camel, O Camel, come out and trot like the rest of us.'

'Humph!' said the Camel; and the Horse went away and told the Man.

Presently the Dog came to him, with a stick in his mouth, and said, 'Camel, O Camel, come and fetch and carry like the rest of us.'

'Humph!' said the Camel; and the Dog went

away and told the Man.

Presently the Ox came to him, with the yoke on his neck, and said, 'Camel, O Camel, come and plough like the rest of us.'

'Humph!' said the Camel; and the Ox went away and told the Man.

At the end of the day the Man called the Horse and the Dog and the Ox together, and said, 'Three, O Three, I'm very sorry for you (with the world so new-and-all); but that Humph-thing in the Desert can't work, or he would have been here by now, so I am going to leave him alone, and you must work double-time to make up for it.'

That made the Three very angry (with the world so new-and-all), and they held a palaver, and an *indaba*, and a *punchayet*, and a pow-wow on the edge of the Desert; and the Camel came chewing milkweed *most* 'scrutiating idle, and laughed at them. Then he said, 'Humph!' and went away again.

Presently there came along the Djinn in charge of All Deserts, rolling in a cloud of dust (Djinns always travel that way because it is Magic), and he stopped to palaver and pow-wow with the Three.

'Djinn of All Deserts,' said the Horse, '*is* it right for any one to be idle, with the world so new-and-all?'

'Certainly not,' said the Djinn.

'Well,' said the Horse, 'there's a thing in the middle of your Howling Desert (and he's a Howler himself) with a long neck and long legs, and he hasn't done a stroke of work since Monday morning. He won't trot.'

'Whew!' said the Djinn, whistling, 'that's my Camel, for all the gold in Arabia! What does he say about it?'

'He says "Humph!" ' said the Dog; 'and he won't fetch and carry.'

'Does he say anything else?'

'Only "Humph!"; and he won't plough,' said the Ox.

'Very good,' said the Djinn. 'I'll humph him if you will kindly wait a minute.'

The Djinn rolled himself up in his dust-cloak, and he took a bearing across the desert, and found the Camel most 'scruciatingly idle, looking at his own reflection in a pool of water.

'My long and bubbling friend,' said the Djinn, 'what's this I hear of your doing no work, with the world so new-and-all?'

'Humph!' said the Camel.

The Djinn sat down, with his chin in his hand, and began to think a Great Magic, while the Camel looked at his own reflection in the pool of water.

'You've given the Three extra work ever since

Monday morning, all on account of your 'scruciating idleness,' said the Djinn; and he went on thinking Magics, with his chin in his hand.

'Humph!' said the Camel.

'I shouldn't say that again if I were you,' said the Djinn; 'you might say it once too often. Bubbles, I want you to work.'

And the Camel said 'Humph!' again; but no sooner had he said it than he saw his back, that he was so proud of, puffing up and puffing up into a great big lolloping humph.

'Do you see that?' said the Djinn. 'That's your very own humph that you've brought upon your very own self by not working. Today is Thursday, and you've done no work since Monday, when the work began. Now you are going to work.'

'How can I,' said the Camel, 'with this humph on my back?'

'That's made a-purpose,' said the Djinn, 'all because you missed those three days. You will be able to work now for three days without eating, because you can live on your humph; and don't you ever say I never did anything for you. Come out of the Desert and go to the Three, and behave. Humph yourself!'

And the Camel humphed himself, humph and all, and went away to join the Three. And from that day to this the Camel always wears a humph (we call it 'hump' now, not to hurt his feelings); but he has never yet caught up with the three days that he missed at the beginning of the world, and he has never yet learned how to behave.

Telephone Troubles

DONALD BISSET

Once upon a time there was a very nice woman and a very nice man. She was called Jenny. He was called George. They had lots of very fine horses and some nice stables and a tiny little office with a telephone and a desk.

They had a big diary on the desk to enter people's names who wanted to come and ride the horses. They had two girls to help them groom the horses, and make the horses' beds, and tidy their stables. One was called Big Sue; and the other was called Little Sue.

Sometimes when people telephoned to the stables to ask if they could come and ride the horses, no one answered the telephone. They were all busy and didn't hear it.

So George thought.

And Little Sue thought.

And Jenny thought.

And Big Sue thought.

Then Jenny had an idea.

43

'What is the use of having our nice horses stomping about their stables, and breathing air, and eating hay and things?' she said. 'Let us teach *them* to answer the telephone.'

'Of course!' said the others. 'What a good idea!'

So Jenny fetched two horses called Burlington and Drumbeat, and said they had to go to telephone school where they would get a lot of

hay to eat, and a lady Supervisor would teach them to answer the telephone.

So George got out the van and drove them to the telephone exchange and promised that he would come and fetch them again in two days. He left them some oats and bran and hay and carrots and gave them each a hug and told them to be good horses, and then said goodbye and came home.

Two days later he fetched them again.

First Burlington took a turn in the office and then Drumbeat. They were very good at answering the phone because the lady at the Exchange had given them a certificate.

But, every day, Jenny noticed that fewer people came to ride their horses.

'Whatever is the matter, George?' she said.

Then – they found out.

Whenever anyone phoned to ask if they could come for a ride, Burlington or Drumbeat always said, 'Neigh!' So people stopped coming.

George and Jenny were very sad. Nobody brought them any money, so they began to cry. And the horses didn't get any hay or oats so they began to cry, too. And Jenny's little girl, Allie, who was six, cried. And Big Sue cried and Little Sue cried.

Soon the stables were under water with all those tears. And Sandy, the dog, and Ginger, the

45

cat, got their feet wet. They did not like getting their feet wet. So they cried, too.

The water got higher and higher, Ginger got on to the roof. And Sandy had to stand on tiptoe with his head up all the time so as not to get his ears wet.

'Jenny,' said George, 'this won't do!'

'No,' said Jenny. 'It won't do, at all!' And she went straight to the office where Drumbeat, who was on duty, was saying, 'Neigh!' in a burbly sort of way, to someone on the telephone. She took him right back to his stable and told him, and Burlington, that they were very good horses, but that they *must not* answer the telephone, any more.

Gradually the water sank and George and Jenny and Little Sue and Big Sue and Allie mopped the place up and dried Sandy and Ginger, and the horses' legs.

Then the telephone rang. Little Sue heard it and answered it, and said, to someone, 'Of course you can come and have a ride.'

Then George fixed a loud telephone bell *outside* the office hut so that they would always hear the phone when it rang. The bell was very loud and one of the horses, whose name was Caspian, almost had a nervous breakdown. So they moved him to a stable a little way off and he soon got quite better. The other horses didn't seem to mind the bell, at all.

After that a lot of people rang up and someone always heard the phone to answer it. So a lot of people came to ride the horses and gave some money to George and Jenny. So they bought the horses lots of nice things to eat, and they all lived happily ever after.

Uncle Charlie's Ramshackle Car

IRIS GRENDER

One day Uncle Charlie came to see us. This time he didn't come by bus or taxi, he came in a brand new car – well, brand new to Uncle Charlie.

We all went outside to admire the new car. Our mother peered inside to see if the seats looked comfortable; our father lifted the bonnet

to inspect the engine; my brother Francis wrote 'Uncle Charlie' in the dust on the boot; and I sat inside and pretended to steer.

'Like it then, do you?' Uncle Charlie asked our mother.

'Well,' she answered, 'it's very nice, but it's a bit ramshackle.'

'What's ramshackle?' Francis and I asked both together.

'Uncle Charlie's car is,' answered our father.

'Never mind that,' said Uncle Charlie. 'She goes like a bird. Go and get ready and I'll take you for a drive in the country.' We hurried indoors and Francis even combed his hair for once.

At last even our mother was ready. She sat in the front seat next to Uncle Charlie, looking as grand as a duchess. Uncle Charlie did whatever drivers do and we began to move. It was lovely driving along our own road in Uncle Charlie's new car. I wished I could see someone to wave to, but there was no one about.

'Now children,' said Uncle Charlie, 'you must learn to play the Car Game. Whenever you see a church you must shout "Allelujah".' As we went round a corner Francis and I both saw a church at the same time. 'Allelujah!' we yelled at the tops of our voices.

'Excellent,' said Uncle Charlie. 'Now when we

go under a bridge you must shout "Hurray".'
Just then we went under a bridge and immediately
afterwards there was a church. So we yelled
'Hurray' and 'Allelujah' without pausing for
breath.

Soon we were out in the country driving along
between green hedges. 'Now,' said Uncle Charlie,
'there's one more thing to learn. When you see a
garage you must shout "Brrm, Brrm, Brrm".'
Francis had a little practice, even though we
didn't pass any garages.

Suddenly the car stopped with a faint choking
sound. 'Oh, dear,' gasped our mother, 'I knew it
would break down. You are terrible, Charlie!
And we're miles from anywhere.'

Uncle Charlie just laughed. 'Let's look on the
bright side, it's not raining.'

Our father sighed and opened the bonnet. He
couldn't see anything wrong with the engine. 'I
think you forgot to put any petrol in, Charlie,' he
said as he closed the bonnet.

Uncle Charlie blushed, bright red right down
to the roots of his hair. Then he said to us,
'Come along children, this will be your first
lesson in pushing a ramshackle car.' Our mother
sat inside and steered. She didn't look so grand
any more. Uncle Charlie, our father, Francis and
I began to push. It was very hard work.

We pushed the car all the way up the hill and

lightly down the other side. Then we all pushed
it along a flat road. We went on for miles and
miles and miles. At last we came to a garage.
'Brrm, Brrm, Brrm,' yelled Francis, remember-
ing the Car Game just in time, and 'Allelujah',
shouted Uncle Charlie, and 'Hurray', shouted
our father.

The next time Uncle Charlie came to take us
out our mother said, 'No thank you, Charlie, I'd
rather catch a bus.' Our father said, 'No thank

you, Charlie, I'd rather walk.' 'Yes please,' said Francis, 'providing I can steer when we break down,' and I said, 'Yes please,' because it was lovely to go for a ride in a car, even if it was ramshackle.

Goldilocks and the Three Bears

RUTH AINSWORTH

Once upon a time, there were three bears. There was a great big father bear, a middle-sized mother bear, and a little baby bear. They lived in a house in a wood.

One morning the Mother Bear made porridge for breakfast and poured it into three bowls. There was a great big bowl for Father Bear, a middle-sized bowl for herself, and a little bowl for Baby Bear. At first the porridge was steaming and much too hot to eat. They did not want to burn their mouths, and they were too polite to blow on it, so they went for a little walk in the wood while their porridge cooled.

That day, a little girl was out for a walk in the same wood. She had golden curls and everybody called her Goldilocks. Sometimes she stopped to pick a flower or to listen to a bird. Soon she came to the house where the three bears lived.

'Oh, what a lovely little house!' said Goldilocks. 'I wonder who lives there?'

She knocked on the door, and as there was no answer she knocked again and again. Then she peeped through the keyhole. But of course the three bears were out for a walk. There was no one to open the door.

'I'll just look inside,' thought Goldilocks. 'No one will mind. They have not even bothered to lock up.' So she opened the door and went in.

The first thing she saw was the bears' three chairs. She climbed into Father Bear's great big chair.

'Oh, it's too hard!' she said.

Then she tried Mother Bear's middle-sized chair.

'Oh, it's too soft!'

Then she sat down in Baby Bear's little chair and she broke the bottom out of it.

Then Goldilocks smelt the delicious smell of the porridge and she saw the three bowls on the table. She was very hungry as she had come out without having any breakfast.

'I'll just have a tiny taste,' she said. 'No one will notice.'

First she tried the porridge in Father Bear's great big bowl. But it was too hot. Next she tried the porridge in Mother Bear's middle-sized bowl. But that was too cold. Then she tried the porridge in Baby Bear's little bowl. It wasn't too hot and it wasn't too cold. It was just right. And

Goldilocks ate up every scrap.

Then Goldilocks thought she would go upstairs and have a nap. She saw the three beds neatly made, Father Bear's great big bed, and Mother Bear's middle-sized bed, and Baby Bear's little bed.

First she lay on the great big bed.

'Oh, that's too hard!'

Then she lay on the middle-sized bed.

'Oh, that's too soft!'

Then she lay on the little bed.

'Oh, it isn't too hard and it isn't too soft. It's just right!'

Goldilocks was so comfortable that she settled down with her head on Baby Bear's pillow and fell fast asleep.

After a while the three bears came back from

their walk, as they thought their porridge would be cool enough to eat. Father Bear saw that his chair had been moved.

'Someone has been sitting on my chair!' he said in a great big voice.

Mother Bear saw that her cushion had been rumpled.

'Someone has been sitting on my chair!' she said in a middle-sized voice.

Then Baby Bear had a look at his chair.

'Someone has been sitting in my chair and has broken the bottom right out!' he said in his little baby voice.

Then they looked at their bowls of porridge on the table. Father Bear saw that his spoon had been moved.

'Someone has been eating my porridge,' he said in a great big voice.

Mother Bear noticed that her spoon had been left in the bowl.

'Someone has been eating my porridge,' she said in a middle-sized voice.

Baby Bear looked at his bowl.

'Someone has been eating my porridge and they've eaten it all up!' he said in a little baby voice.

'Let's go upstairs and look at the bedrooms,' said Father Bear, and they all went upstairs. Father Bear saw that his blanket was rumpled.

'Someone has been lying on my bed!' he said, in his great big voice.

Mother Bear saw that her pillow was dented.

'Someone has been lying on my bed!' she said, in a middle-sized voice.

Then Baby Bear looked at his bed.

'Someone has been lying on my bed and she's lying there still!' he said, in a little baby voice.

Now when Father Bear was speaking his growly voice sounded deep like thunder, and Goldilocks took no notice. When Mother Bear was speaking in her middle-sized voice it sounded like the wind in the trees, and Goldilocks took no notice. But when Baby Bear spoke in his shrill baby voice it went right through her head. She woke, and sat up in bed. She was very surprised to see three strange bears looking down at her.

She was out of bed in a twinkling, and down the stairs, and out of the door, and she never stopped running till she got back to her own home. She had such a fright that she never went for a walk in the wood again to look for the little house.

Don't Blame Me!

RICHARD HUGHES

There was one a young man called Simon, who
lived a long way from where he worked. So he
thought, 'If I could only buy a nice motor-bike
to go to my work on, that would be fine.' So
Simon saved up his money, till he thought he
had nearly enough; and one Saturday he went
off to the street where second-hand motor-bikes
were sold, to see if he could find one to suit
him.

At almost the first shop he came to, there was
a most grand-looking motor-bike, almost new;
and the price the man was asking seemed much
too cheap for such a fine one. So Simon said he
would buy it; but all the man said was, 'Don't
blame me!' – which seemed to Simon a funny
thing to say.

Simon bought it, and rode it home; and it
went sweetly and well, and he was very pleased
with it. So on Monday morning he started out
on it to his work; and as he went he wondered

what the man who sold it meant when he said, 'Don't blame me!'

Simon knew soon enough, though; for as he was riding along a lonely piece of road, he felt the motor-bike beginning to wriggle under him, as if it was coming to bits. It wasn't doing that, but it was doing something far worse – it was turning into a crocodile!

When Simon found he was riding a crocodile, he was more frightened than he had ever been before. He was too frightened to stay on its back; so he jumped off, and began to run for his life with the crocodile after him; and at first he left the crocodile a bit behind.

But presently Simon began to get so tired that the crocodile began to catch him up, and he thought he would have to give up and be eaten. Just then he saw a donkey in the road before him. He managed to run till he had caught up with the donkey, and then he said:

'Mr Donkey, will you kindly give me a ride?'

But the donkey was a selfish one, not a nice donkey at all; and just because he saw Simon was really tired and needed a ride, he said, No, he wouldn't.

'You can jolly well walk,' he said. '*I* have to!'

'All right,' said Simon; 'then let me pass you,' for the road was rather narrow.

So the donkey let him pass; and Simon

walked. Now that he had the donkey in between him and the crocodile he didn't feel quite so frightened; so he didn't trouble to walk very fast.

Presently the donkey said:

'Hee-haw! Hee-haw! Simon, Simon, will you walk a little faster? There's a crocodile behind me, and he's snapped off my tail.'

But Simon wouldn't trouble to walk faster, and the donkey couldn't pass him to get away from the crocodile; so presently the donkey said:

'Hee-haw! Hee-haw! HEE-HAW! *Will* you walk a little faster, *please?* There's a crocodile behind me, and he's swallowed me all but my head.'

But even then Simon wouldn't trouble to walk any faster; and then at last he heard the donkey say in a faint, small voice:

'Hee-haw! Hee-haw! I'm *inside* the crocodile now!'

So then Simon knew he would have to run again, so away he went for his life, with the crocodile after him. But because he had had a good rest, at first he left the crocodile behind; and also, of course, the crocodile had a heavy donkey inside him now.

Presently in the road ahead of him Simon saw a giant.

'Mr Giant,' said Simon to the giant, 'will you kindly give me a ride!'

'Certainly!' said the giant kindly. 'Certainly, certainly, certainly!' So he picked up Simon and sat him on his shoulder, and went on strolling along the road, swinging his umbrella as he went.

Presently Simon saw the crocodile catching them up; but he didn't tell the giant, because he didn't quite know what to say.

'Ow!' the giant cried suddenly, and began to dance. 'I've been stung by a wasp!'

When the giant danced it was difficult for Simon to hold on; but somehow he managed, and looking down he saw what had really happened. It wasn't a wasp, it was the crocodile who had bitten the giant, and who was holding on to the seat of the giant's trousers like grim death.

But the giant couldn't see that, because it was behind him and his neck was stiff. He just kept on dancing and swishing behind him with his umbrella. And though Simon was sorry to have got the kind giant into so much trouble, he wasn't going to let go. He just hung on and hoped for the best.

At last, by great good luck, the giant managed to hit the crocodile with his umbrella. Now, giants' umbrellas are generally magic, and this one certainly was. For no sooner did it touch the crocodile, than the crocodile turned back again into a motor-bike, and just then Simon lost hold of the giant's collar and fell in the road with a frightful thump on his head.

The thump knocked him silly at first, but presently he sat up and opened his eyes. There was the motor-bike lying in the road; a crowd of people was standing around.

'That's a nice motor-bike you've got,' said one of them. 'Do you want to sell it?'

'Yes,' said Simon.

'Then I'll buy it,' said the other chap.

'All right,' said Simon, 'buy it if you like, but *don't blame me!*'

For Simon saw then what none of the others saw. He saw the motor-bike open its mouth and grin with all its wicked white teeth. And no wonder the motor-bike was pleased! For the young man who had bought it now was fat and juicy, and didn't look as if *he* could run an inch!

Gilbert the Ostrich

JANE HOLIDAY

The Dancer family lived in an ordinary house. Mr Dancer was ordinary. Mrs Dancer was ordinary. Martin and Donna were ordinary children. And Conker was an ordinary dog – black and white with a wagging tail. So how did they come to have an *ostrich* living with them? Nobody knew.

Anyway, the ostrich *was* living there and his name was Gilbert. Gilbert was a handsome bird with a small head, a fluffy body, long legs and big, brown eyes. He was so tall he could change all the light bulbs in the house without standing on a chair *but* he dropped them SMASH on the floor.

Everyone said what a lovely bird Gilbert was, but he had some nasty habits. He ate nuts and bolts. He ate jam jar lids. He ate the bathroom plug. He ate thirty pence left on the kitchen table. He ate the top of Donna's fountain-pen. She could still write with it, so she didn't mind.

He ate the laces of Martin's football boots. Martin *did* mind. He shouted at Gilbert, 'You're a nasty, greedy bird!'

Gilbert was sad. He didn't know it was wrong to eat bootlaces.

In some ways Gilbert was very good. He drank all his milk up. Every morning, Mrs Dancer said, 'Drink all your milk, Martin,' and 'Drink your milk, Donna.' Martin and Donna always said, 'Ugh!' but Gilbert had finished every drop.

He could run very fast too. So Mrs Dancer sent him to the shops. He carried the shopping-basket on his wing. In the basket was the shopping-list and some money. Sometimes, too, he helped clean the house. He could reach up to the ceiling and dust the cobwebs away.

Everyone liked Gilbert. He was such a *polite* bird.

One afternoon Mr and Mrs Dancer took Martin and Donna to the cinema. They left Gilbert at home. Last time he went he had eaten two ashtrays. Now there was a big notice outside the cinema. It read:

NO OSTRICHES.

Mrs Dancer was worried about leaving Gilbert. 'I hope he doesn't feel hungry.'

Mr Dancer was worried too. 'I hope he doesn't feel lonely.'

Martin and Donna were glad he wasn't coming. They always had to sit in the back row when Gilbert came, because he was so tall.

'Be a good bird, Gilbert,' said Mrs Dancer. She left him a pint of milk and some cheese. Mr Dancer left him an old screwdriver. Martin and Donna left him some marbles.

When they came home at six o'clock, Gilbert was fast asleep in an armchair.

'He's drunk the milk,' said Mrs Dancer.

'He's eaten the cheese,' said Mr Dancer, 'and half the screwdriver.'

'And all the marbles,' said Martin and Donna.

Those weren't the only things Gilbert had eaten.

'I can't get into the bathroom,' called Martin.

67

'We can't get into the bedrooms,' called Mrs Dancer and Donna.

Do you know *why* they couldn't? Gilbert had eaten *all* the dooknobs. He hadn't left a single one anywhere. He'd even eaten the knob on the oven door. Mr Dancer managed to open one door with some tools. Then he opened the other doors.

They didn't have new door knobs put on though. Now all the doors in the Dancers' house are *swing* doors. You *push* them open. They *swing* to behind you. Everyone liked them better, and said that Gilbert was a good bird really.

I wonder what he will eat next. Do you?

The Selfish Giant

OSCAR WILDE
RETOLD BY ALLISON REED

There was once a giant who came down from the mountains to build himself a castle in the valley. All the people of the valley were amazed by the beauty of his castle and the garden that surrounded it. Flowers of every scent and colour grew there, and birds and butterflies flew everywhere. It seemed there was magic in the garden and in the afternoons after school the children would go there to play.

One day the giant dug up a tree as a present and set off up the steep mountain path to visit his friend. His friend was delighted to see him and the two giants sat talking for days and days. The giant told his friend all about his wonderful garden.

'But surely,' his friend said, 'it cannot be the most beautiful garden in the world if you let all the children trample on it.'

And the giant saw some sense in what his friend said.

The next day the giants climbed to the very top of the mountain and found the biggest boulder anyone had ever seen.

'This will build a fine wall,' his friend said. And the giant set off home struggling under the weight of the enormous boulder.

After many days the giant reached the valley. With his left hand he smashed the great stone and laid the pieces one upon the other to build a great wall around the garden. It was autumn by the time the wall was finished. The giant stood back to admire his work and thought, 'Now it really is my garden. No one will be able to spoil it.'

Outside the garden, the children had nowhere to play. They wandered round the high walls when their lessons were over and talked about the beautiful garden inside.

'How happy we were there,' they said to each other.

Winter came, and the garden was bleak and white and silent. The giant stared at the snow and longed for spring.

Months went by and there was no sign of a thaw. Little did the giant know that outside his wall the sun shone and the grass was green. Then one morning, the giant was woken by the song of a bird.

'At last,' he cried, 'spring is here.' He looked out of the window and saw that the snow was melting. In a corner of the garden the children had made a hole in his great wall. Laughing and shouting they ran happily into the garden. Everything came to life again. Flowers bloomed and the grass was green.

The giant hurried down to greet the children but when they saw him coming they ran away to hide. Only the smallest boy remained. He stood crying under a tree whose branches still had no leaves. The giant gently lifted him up and as the boy's small hands touched the branches the tree burst into blossom. 'How selfish I have been,' thought the giant. 'With my great wall I have

locked the spring out of my garden.'

The children who had been watching came out from their hiding places. They shyly gathered round the giant and offered him flowers.

'It is your garden now children,' said the giant.

And together they started to break down the great wall. With the stones they built arches and the children ran round and round and in and out of them.

The giant saw that his garden was more beautiful than ever. He loved all the children but he kept a special place in his heart for the smallest child. For it was he who had shown the giant how his selfishness had destroyed his garden. From that day until the end of the giant's life the children played happily in the garden.

Big Roar and Little Roar

DONALD BISSET

Once upon a time there was a lion who could only roar little roars. His name was Sam.

'Now, go out into the jungle, Sam,' said his mother, 'and roar with the other lions.'

So Sam went into the jungle and all the other lions roared very loud, 'ROOOARR!!'

'Now you roar, Sam!' they said. And Sam went, 'Roar! Roar!'

All the other lions laughed at him.

So Sam went home and took some cough mixture to help him roar better. Then he went into the back garden and practised his roaring.

But no matter how hard he tried, he could only roar little roars.

He did feel sad!

He went into the jungle and met his friend Jack, who was the best roarer in the world.

Jack could roar so loudly that trees trembled when they heard him and clouds scurried away and animals ran and hid. Even the King in his

castle was afraid.

'There's Jack roaring again!' he said to the Queen. 'What a noise he makes! I say, my dear, don't you think he would make a very good guard on the front door, so that no one could come and steal the crown jewels? There's only a cat and a mouse guarding them at the moment.'

'That's a good idea!' said the Queen.

So the King told the Prime Minister to go and ask Jack to come to the Castle and guard the crown jewels.

'And ask him to baby-sit,' too!' said the Queen.

The Prime Minister went into the jungle. When he saw Jack, he was afraid and climbed a tree.

'The King says will you please come to the Castle and guard the crown jewels?' he said. 'And the Queen says would you please baby-sit, sometimes?'

Jack was very pleased and went to the Castle with the Prime Minister. When they got there, the King said, 'Now, you sit outside the front gate and roar.'

So Jack roared:

'ROOOAR!! ROOOAR!!'

'That *is* a good roar,' said the King.

But the Queen wasn't pleased.

'Every time he roars he wakes the baby,' she said. 'I will not put up with it.'

She looked out of the window.

'You are very naughty!' she said. 'You roar so loudly you wake the baby.'

Jack thought for a moment. Then he went into the jungle and met his friend Sam, and told him to come to the castle and roar, too.

So Sam came and roared little roars:

'Roar! Roar!'

The Queen was very pleased.

'That's very good!' she said. 'When the baby's awake, Jack can be on guard and roar as loud as he likes. And when the baby's asleep Sam can be on guard and roar little roars.'

Sam and Jack were very pleased and danced for joy.

Since the baby was asleep just then, Jack went down to the kitchen and the cook gave him his dinner. And Sam stayed on guard and roared little roars:

'Roar! Roar!'

'You *are* a good lion, Sam!' said the Queen.

The Great Gulper

JIM AND CHRISTOPHER SLATER

One day a small brown monster popped out of an oil pipe.

Mr Grim who owned a zoo came by helicopter to take the monster away.

Mr Grim put the monster in a cage which had iron bars and glass all around the outside.

'He doesn't look much, does he?' he said to the keepers.

'He seems very friendly, sir,' the oldest keeper said.

'You can look after him then,' Mr Grim snapped.

Fred was the keeper all the animals liked most. He was very kind and could really talk to them.

After a few days Fred went to see Mr A. Mazing.

'You know all about monsters,' he said. 'Please tell me about this one.'

'He's a young Gulper,' Mr A. Mazing replied.

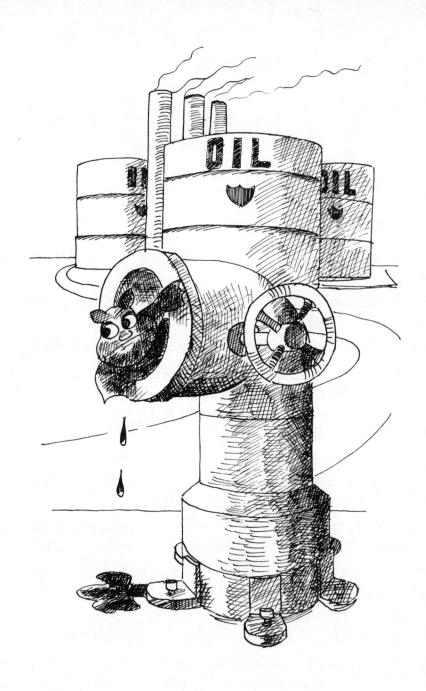

'He needs to drink one gallon of oil every day.'

Thousands of people came to see the little monster. The Gulper was very friendly and sometimes stood on his head and turned cart-wheels to make the crowd laugh.

Some of the children loved the Gulper even more than the Panda.

Fred became very proud of his monster.

As the Gulper grew up he began to need more oil and was soon drinking five gallons a day.

When Mr Grim found out he was very angry.

'The Gulper costs too much to keep,' he said. 'From now on, don't give him more than one gallon a day.'

'That won't be enough,' Fred replied. 'Unless he has five gallons a day, the Gulper will die.'

The Gulper became ill and shrank to half the size he was when he first arrived at Grim's Zoo.

Then one morning Fred read in his newspaper that a tanker had crashed on the rocks just off the South Coast of England.

'Thousands of gallons of oil are drifting towards Brighton and Bournemouth,' the newspaper read.

'I know,' Fred said to himself. 'I'll take the

Gulper down to Brighton and give him a big drink of oil.'

Fred didn't tell Mr Grim about his plan.

That night he took the Gulper down to Brighton in his car.

When Fred wasn't looking a big wave swept the little monster out to sea, but as soon as he smelt oil he began to swim towards it.

When the Gulper reached the oil he drank in great gulps, going backwards and forwards until it had all gone.

When the Gulper swam back to the shore Fred was there waiting for him.

'Oh, there you are,' Fred said with a smile. 'I was so worried about you.'

The Gulper smiled back at Fred. He was full of oil and very happy.

That night Mr Grim sacked Fred and wouldn't let the Gulper return to his zoo. The little monster slept in the spare room of Fred's small flat in London.

The following morning, as a special treat, Fred let the Gulper have breakfast in bed.

'I don't know how I'm going to be able to keep you,' Fred said. 'That came from the last can of oil that I use for my car.'

The Gulper smiled back at Fred to let him know that he understood.

Fred went to buy his morning newspaper and

to his surprise found a photograph of the Gulper on the front page.

In big black print there were three words:

MONSTER SAVES BRITAIN

Someone must have taken a picture of the Gulper when he was drinking all the oil. The little monster had become a hero.

All that day people kept coming to see the Gulper to take more pictures and hear the story from Fred. Even Mr Grim telephoned.

'Would you and the Gulper like to come back to Grim's Zoo?' he asked in his nicest voice.

'No thanks,' Fred replied. 'The Gulper's much happier here with me.'

In the evening the Gulper went on the television news and everyone in England was soon talking about the little monster.

A week later the Gulper went to Buckingham Palace where the Queen gave him a medal.

Afterwards the Queen asked Fred and the Gulper to have tea with her. The Gulper only wanted more oil, but Fred knew the little monster was very polite so he said: 'Thank you very much, Your Majesty.'

For tea, the Queen, Fred and the Gulper had some sandwiches. To his surprise Fred could see that the Gulper liked them a lot.

'What are the sandwiches, Your Majesty?' Fred asked.

'Marmite!' the Queen replied.

And that was how Fred found out that the Gulper liked Marmite sandwiches.

Now Fred and the Gulper live in a big house overlooking Hyde Park.

The Gulper has Marmite sandwiches every day unless a tanker crashes. Then the little monster swims out to sea and has a big drink of oil.

Nowadays most people call the little monster the Great Gulper.

You can often see him riding through Hyde Park, weaing his top hat and medal. If you do – give him a friendly wave. Remember the Great Gulper saved Britain.

Little Old Mrs Pepperpot

ALF PRØYSEN

There was once an old woman who went to bed at night as old women usually do, and in the morning she woke up as old women usually do. But on this particular morning she found herself shrunk to the size of a pepperpot, and old women don't usually do that. The odd thing was, her name really was Mrs Pepperpot.

'Well, as I'm now the size of a pepperpot, I shall have to make the best of it,' she said to herself, for she had no one else to talk to; her husband was out in the fields and all her children were grown up and gone away.

Now she happened to have a great deal to do that day. First of all she had to clean the house, then there was all the washing which was lying in soak and waiting to be done, and lastly she had to make pancakes for supper.

'I must get out of bed somehow,' she thought, and, taking hold of a corner of the eiderdown, she started rolling herself up in it. She rolled and rolled until the eiderdown was like a huge sausage, which fell softly on the floor. Mrs Pepperpot crawled out and she hadn't hurt herself a bit.

The first job was to clean the house, but that was quite easy; she just sat down in front of a mouse-hole and squeaked till the mouse came out.

'Clean the house from top to bottom,' she said, 'or I'll tell the cat about you.' So the mouse cleaned the house from top to bottom.

Mrs Pepperpot called the cat: 'Puss! Puss! Lick out all the plates and dishes or I'll tell the dog about you.' And the cat licked all the plates and dishes clean.

Then the old woman called the dog. 'Listen, dog; you make the bed and open the window and I'll give you a bone as a reward.' So the dog did as he was told, and when he had finished he sat down on the front doorstep and waved his tail so hard he made the step shine like a mirror.

'You'll have to get the bone yourself,' said Mrs Pepperpot. 'I haven't time to wait on people.' She pointed to the window-sill where a large bone lay.

After this she wanted to start her washing. She had put it to soak in the brook, but the brook was almost dry. So she sat down and started muttering in a discontented sort of way: 'I have lived a long time, but in all my born days I never saw the brook so dry. If we don't have a shower soon, I expect everyone will die of thirst.' Over and over again she said it, all the time looking up at the sky.

At last the raincloud in the sky got so angry that it decided to drown the old woman altogether. But she crawled under a monk's-hood flower, where she stayed snug and warm while the rain poured down and rinsed her clothes clean in the brook.

Now the old woman started muttering again: 'I have lived a long time, but in all my born days I have never known such a feeble South Wind as we have had lately. I'm sure if the South Wind started blowing this minute it couldn't lift me off the ground, even though I am no bigger than a pepperpot.'

The South Wind heard this and instantly came tearing along, but Mrs Pepperpot hid in an empty badger set, and from there she watched the South Wind blow all the clothes right up on to her clothes-line.

Again she started muttering: 'I have lived a long time, but in all my born days I have never seen the sun give so little heat in the middle of the summer. It seems to have lost all its power, that's a fact.'

When the sun heard this it turned scarlet with rage and sent down fiery rays to give the old woman sunstroke. But by this time she was safely back in her house, and was sailing about the sink in a saucer. Meanwhile the furious sun dried all the clothes on the line.

'Now for cooking the supper,' said Mrs Pepperpot; 'my husband will be back in an hour and, by hook or by crook, thirty pancakes must be ready on the table.'

She had mixed the dough for the pancakes in a bowl the day before. Now she sat down beside the bowl and said: 'I have always been fond of you, bowl, and I've told all the neighbours that there's not a bowl like you anywhere. I am sure, if you really wanted to, you could walk straight over to the cooking-stove and turn it on.'

And the bowl went straight over to the stove and turned it on.

Then Mrs Pepperpot said: 'I'll never forget the day I bought my frying-pan. There were lots of pans in the shop, but I said: "If I can't have that pan hanging right over the shop assistant's head, I won't buy any pan at all. For that is the best pan in the whole world, and I'm sure if I were ever in trouble that pan could jump on to the stove by itself." '

And there and then the frying-pan jumped on to the stove. And when it was hot enough, the bowl tilted itself to let the dough run on to the pan.

Then the old woman said: 'I once read a fairy-tale about a pancake which could roll along the road. It was the stupidest story that ever I read. But I'm sure the pancake on the pan could easily turn a somersault in the air if it really wanted to.'

At this the pancake took a great leap from sheer pride and turned a somersault as Mrs Pepperpot had said. Not only one pancake, but *all* the pancakes did this, and the bowl went on tilting and the pan went on frying until, before the hour was up, there were thirty pancakes on the dish.

Then Mr Pepperpot came home. And, just as he opened the door, Mrs Pepperpot turned back to her usual size. So they sat down and ate their supper.

And the old woman said nothing about having been as small as a pepperpot, because old women don't usually talk about such things.

Acknowledgements

The compiler and publisher wish to thank the following for permission to use copyright material in this anthology:

David Higham Associates Ltd for 'The Elephant's Picnic' and 'Don't Blame Me' from *The Wonder Dog* by Richard Hughes, published by Chatto and Windus

Associated Book Publishers Ltd for 'Charlie Finds a Pet' from *Charlie, Emma and Alberic* by Margaret Greaves, published by Methuen Children's Books

Hodder and Stoughton Children's Books for 'The Billy-Goats Gruff' from *Folk Tales* retold by Leila Berg

Harrap Ltd for 'The Little Wooden Horse' by Ursula Moray Williams

A P Watt Ltd for 'How the Camel got its Hump' from *The Just So Stories* by Rudyard Kipling

A M Heath & Company Ltd for 'Big Roar and Little Roar' from *Talks With a Tiger* by Donald Bisset, published by Methuen Children's Books

Beaver Books Ltd for 'Telephone Troubles' from *This is Ridiculous* by Donald Bisset

William Heinemann Ltd for 'Goldlilocks and the Three Bears' from *Three Bags Full* by Ruth Ainsworth

Granada Publishing Ltd for 'The Great Gulper' by Jim and Christopher Slater from Amazing Monster Series

Jane Holiday for 'Gilbert the Ostrich' from *Stories from Listen with Mother* published by Hutchinson Children's Books Ltd

Marjorie Stannard for 'Thomas and the Monster' from *More Stories from Listen with Mother* published by Hutchinson Children's Books Ltd

Eugenie Summerfield for 'Wriggly Worm and the New Pet' from *Animal Tales from Listen with Mother* published by Hutchinson Children's Books Ltd